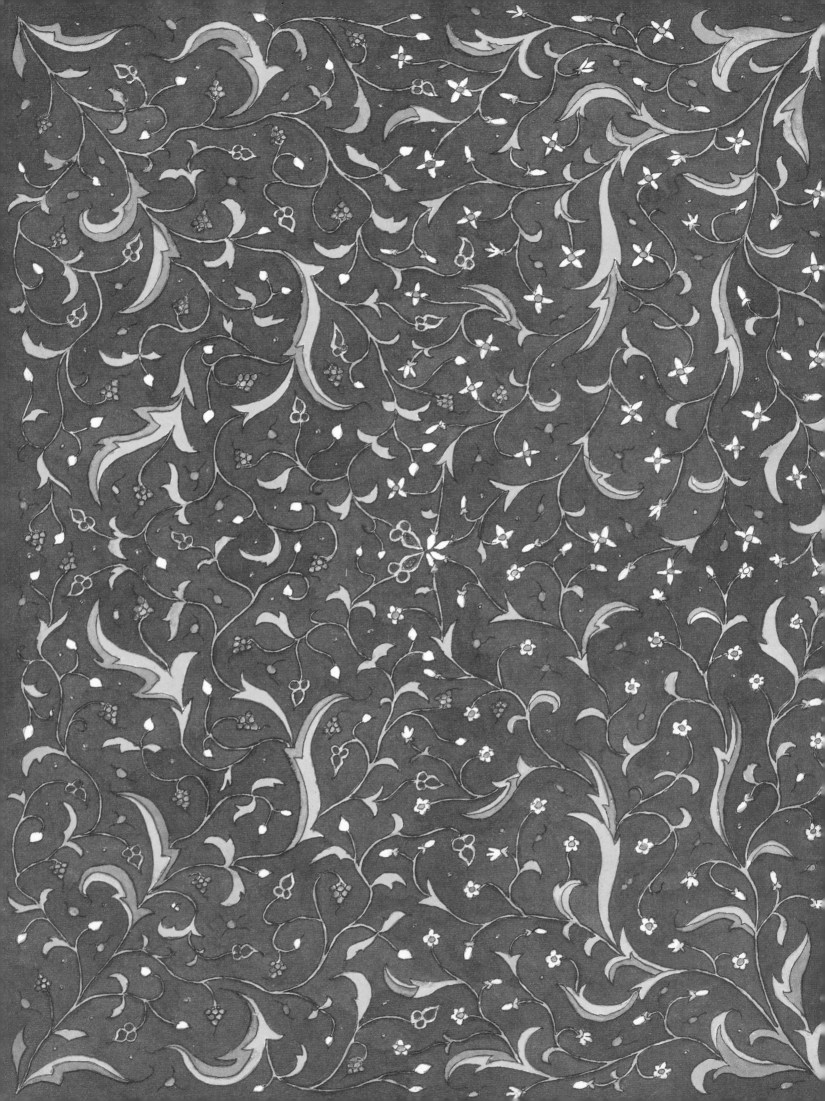

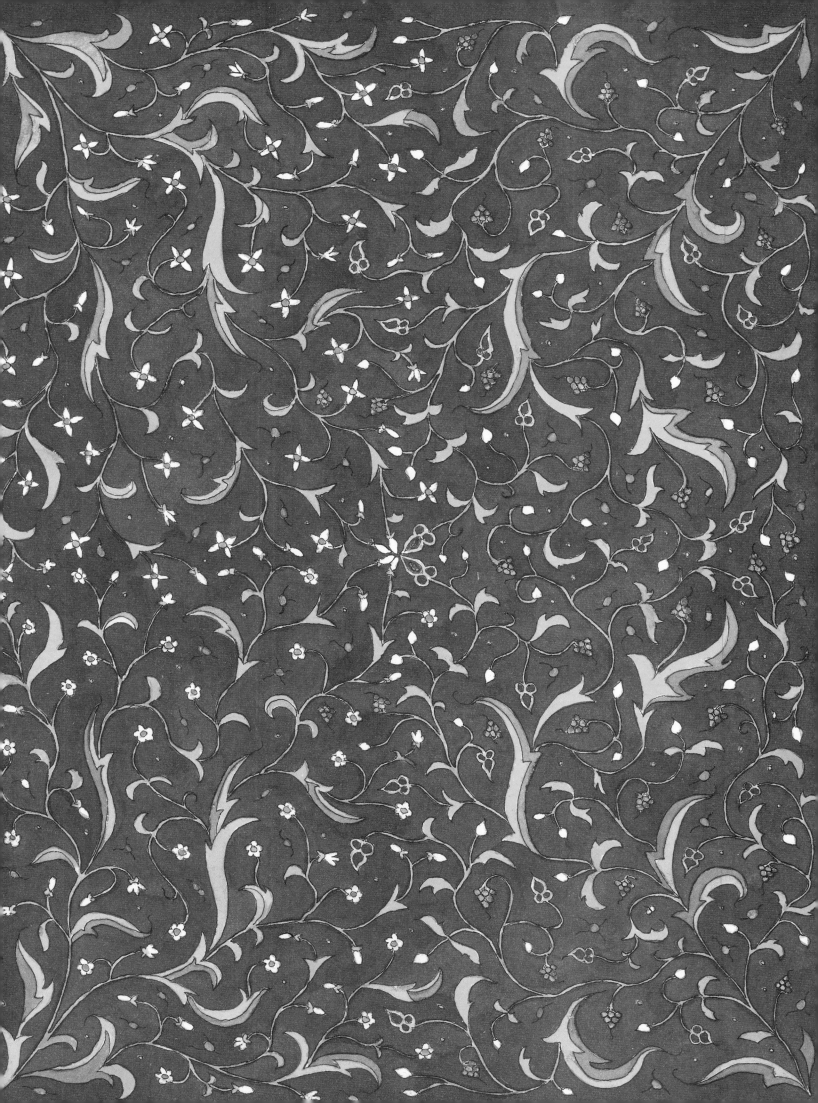

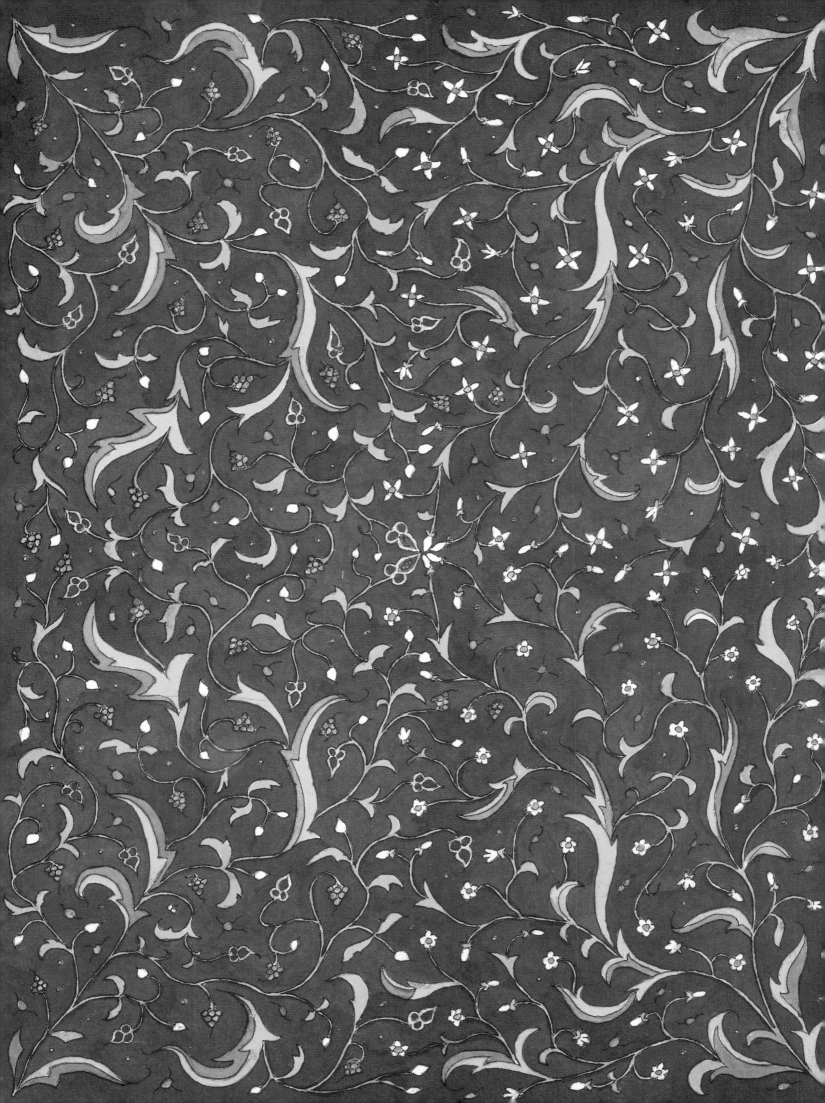

Illuminations

ALADDIN BOOKS
Macmillan Publishing Company   New York
Maxwell Macmillan Canada   Toronto
Maxwell Macmillan International
New York   Oxford   Singapore   Sydney

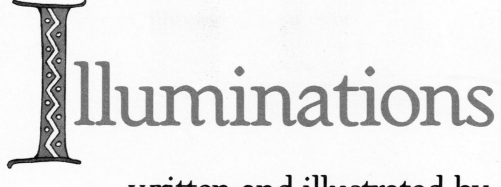

Illuminations

written and illustrated by

Jonathan Hunt

For Lisa

FIRE △ WATER ▽ EARTH GOLD

MERCURY ASHES IRON SAND

Alchemist

Alchemy is the foundation of the modern science of chemistry. Alchemists often dedicated their lives to trying to uncover the natural laws of the universe. These early scientists believed that certain ordinary metals could be transformed into gold through a combination of science and magic. Many alchemists also believed in the possibility of immortality and tried to distill the elixir of life—a drink that would grant everlasting life.

Black Death • The Black Death, or bubonic plague, had a widespread and lasting effect on the fabric of medieval life. The disease was carried by fleas which, in turn, were carried by rats. Merchant ships with rat-infested holds may have been responsible for the spread of the Black Death to Europe from the Far East. Scholars estimate that between 1347 and 1350 one out of every three people in western Europe died.

Coat of Arms

• The use of a coat of arms, or heraldic shield, began in the second half of the twelfth century. Each knight wore a symbolic animal or design ◇ on his surcoat and painted on his shield so that he could be recognized in the heat of battle. Traditional family coats of arms were passed down to succeeding generations. • 🐉 • The lion was a popular heraldic symbol and has been used by the English royal family since the reign of Richard I (1189–1199).

Dragon

Dragon ◆ Dragons are mythical creatures that come in many shapes, sizes, and temperaments. Some people blamed fire-breathing dragons for the destruction of crops and cities, and various other calamities. These mysterious, winged serpents were reputed to spend most of their long lives guarding their secret hoards of jewels and stealing cattle from nearby farms. The dragon was another popular heraldic symbol.

Excalibur ◇

Some say Excalibur was the sword King Arthur pulled from the stone to establish his right to the British throne. Others say that Excalibur was King Arthur's second sword, given to him by the Lady of the Lake. Excalibur was powerful and mighty, but its scabbard, or sheath, was even more valuable, for it protected its bearer from harm. Upon the death of the great king, Excalibur was returned to the Lady of the Lake.

Falconry

Hunting for food was a necessity in the Middle Ages. It was also the foundation of many popular sports among the wealthy. In falconry, a falconer trained birds of prey, usually peregrine falcons, to hunt and kill small birds and animals. Bells were attached to the falcon's feet so that the bird could be located by its owner. The falconer also kept his falcon hooded so that it would remain calm until the hunt began.

Grail ◆ The grail, a mysterious vessel or cup, has many meanings in medieval art and literature. In Christian times, the grail was identified with the chalice that was used at the Last Supper. ❖❖❖❖❖❖ Some of King Arthur's knights dedicated their lives to the quest for the Holy Grail. This fabulous relic, however, revealed its great mysteries to only the purest knight in the world, Sir Galahad. ◆◆◆◆◆◆

Herald ◆ The herald was originally an announcer at tournaments. As the Middle Ages progressed, the herald evolved into an important and dignified figure. Heralds recorded battlefield heroics, determined how men became knights, and regulated the symbols used on coats of arms. Each symbol suggested a different meaning and rank, and it was the herald's duty to keep this heraldic code in good order. There are four chief heralds, or kings of arms, in Britain today.

Illumination

An illumination is a picture, design, or decoration drawn on a manuscript page. In the Middle Ages, illuminators embellished handwritten texts with gold, silver, and colors. Some illuminators were monks, others were professional painters, both women and men. Their miniature pictures added interest, and they were helpful in telling the story. A well-known illuminated manuscript is the Irish Book of Kells.

Joust

A joust was a contest between two knights on horseback. The knights rode at each other with lances and shields and tried to knock each other to the ground.

A joust could also be a form of "trial by combat," in which a man accused of a crime might prove his innocence by victory. Several jousts comprised a tournament, and the victorious knight was often granted great honors and prizes.

 Knight ◆ The role of the knight in medieval society developed over time. The earliest knights included any man able to acquire armor, a weapon, and a horse. In later times, knights were chivalrous men-at-arms, faithful servants to their king, lord, or lady. ▰ A young man served as a page and then squire before he was dubbed a knight and granted a parcel of land, called a fief. The legendary knights of the Round Table were role models for every aspiring knight.

Lord • The feudal lord ruled over a section of land that was chartered to him by the king. The lord, in turn, granted fiefs to his knights and sublet smaller parcels of land to his serfs, or villeins. ◆ On these estates the lords built castles, which were both mighty fortresses and symbols of power.

Merlin

The legendary Merlin was a great enchanter. Many think that he supervised the building of Stonehenge. The powerful wizard helped to raise Arthur Pendragon to be king of England, and he was Arthur's most trusted advisor. Some books say Merlin was imprisoned—in a tree, rock, or cave—by his wily pupil, Vivianne. Others say that Merlin retreated to Bardsay Island, where he guards the Thirteen Treasures of Britain and awaits King Arthur's return.

Normans

The Norman people spread from northern France to subdue England in the eleventh century. William the Conqueror 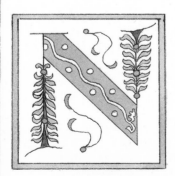 used his English prisoners to build fortresses: wooden towers called baileys perched atop man-made hills called mottes. These fortified structures gradually evolved into what we now call castles.

Oriflamme

The oriflamme was originally the sacred banner of the Abbey of St. Denis—a monastery near Paris. That banner was red or orange-red and usually flown from a lance.

The oriflamme later became the Royal Standard, or flag, of the king of France, and it was carried at the head of the king's forces whenever they met another army in battle.

Portcullis

A portcullis was a heavy wooden grille that could be raised and lowered to seal off and protect the main gateway to a castle or fortified town.

The entire outside face of the portcullis was clad with iron for additional strength. The vertical timbers were pointed at the bottom and capped with iron. The portcullis was also a symbol in heraldry.

Quintain

The quintain was used in sport and in training for agility. In its most basic form, the quintain was a vertical post with a freely swinging crossbar. On one end of the horizontal bar was a shield, and on the other, a weight, such as a heavy sack. The knight-in-training rode at the quintain and struck the shield with his lance. If he did not duck in time, the sack swung about and knocked him from the saddle.

Round Table

The Order of the Round Table was established by King Arthur under the guidance of Merlin. Arthur's knights gathered at a round table. The shape of the table signified the equal importance of each knight.  Accounts of the table's size vary, but most experts agree that one place at the table, the Perilous Seat, was left vacant. Only the true and pure knight of the grail could sit in the Perilous Seat, and this turned out to be Sir Galahad.

Scribe

Medieval books were rare and costly. Books, letters, and laws were hand-copied by scribes. Most lords and ladies hired a scribe as a secretary to draw up a dictated letter or decree. Hot wax was then dripped onto the parchment and the lord or lady pressed a personal seal, called a signet, into the wax as proof of authorship.

Troubadour ◆ Troubadours were lyric poets, traveling musicians, and storytellers. During the Middle Ages, they wandered through southern France, northern Italy, and eastern Spain. Troubadours were sometimes hired to entertain lords and ladies with grand tales of love, chivalrous knights, and distant lands.

Unicorn

The mythical unicorn looks like a horse with a single horn protruding from its forehead. This horn was believed to have magical and healing qualities. The unicorn represented chastity and purity, and it appeared again and again in the paintings, tapestries, stained glass windows, and literature of the time, as well as in heraldry.

Villein

 The villeins, or serfs, were common people who lived and worked on parcels of land sublet to them by the lord. The villein worked three days for himself, three days for his lord, and rested on the Sabbath. Men and women were born to this lowly position, or arrived at it when they refused to go to war or had to work off a debt.

Wattle and Daub

 Some houses and shops in the Middle Ages were constructed of wattle and daub. This means that the main frame of the building consisted of hardwood posts and beams, and the spaces between them were filled with woven mats of grass and reeds called wattle.

The wattle was, in turn, covered with mud or clay called daub.

Xylography

Xylography is not a medieval word, but it describes a medieval art called woodcut—engraving a picture or design into a block of wood. Ink was then rolled onto the block and it was pressed against parchment or paper to create multiple copies of the same image.

Printing books by woodcut was difficult, and the earliest printers of the Middle Ages, among them Johannes Gutenberg and William Caxton, eagerly experimented with movable type.

Yoke ◆ A yoke was a device that was placed around the neck of a horse or ox so that the animal could be hooked up to a wagon or plow. 🌿 🌿 🌿 🌿 🌿 🌿 🌿
When villeins used oxen, they plowed long narrow strips of land because it took more time and effort to turn the stubborn animals around than it did to urge them the extra distance. 🌿 🌿 The yoke is still used in some parts of the world.

Zither

The most popular form of the zither in the Middle Ages was called a psaltery. It was a stringed instrument consisting of a shallow wooden sound box over which were stretched five melody strings and as many as forty accompaniment strings. A psaltery was usually laid flat on a table or the musician's lap and plucked with a plectrum or strummed with the fingers.

A NOTE FROM THE AUTHOR

Some of the finest showcases of medieval life are the illuminated manuscripts left to us by the generations of scribes and monks who labored their entire lives to preserve and create new copies of existing texts. Many of these manuscripts have survived because of their religious significance. The decorations, or miniatures, that the illuminators added to the hand-lettered text mirrored the architecture, clothing, and life-styles of medieval Europe.

I have chosen to do this book in a format that reflects these early illuminated manuscripts. I have also chosen to present scenes from everyday life as well as scenes inspired by the legends of the time. Opinions differ, but most historians agree that the daunting time period known as the Middle Ages falls between the sack of Rome in A.D. 410 and the emergence of the Renaissance in the late 1400s. That's about a thousand years.

Of course, it would be impossible to condense the wide scope of this turbulent time into twenty-six words and pictures. Many things can happen and change in a thousand years. But I hope that, as an introduction, *Illuminations* will tempt you to discover more about the Middle Ages.

ABOUT THE ART

The artwork in this book was first rendered in black ink and then colored with transparent watercolors. Certain paintings mean more than they may seem to at first glance.

For example, you may have noticed that in the upper right corner of the painting for alchemist, there is a parchment covered with strange symbols. Alchemy was a risky business, and many alchemists were accused of practicing witchcraft. To avoid this terrible fate, alchemists disguised their formulas by using these and other secret symbols and codes.

I had a lot of fun creating my own shield for the coat of arms painting. The shield that you see is a good example of symbolism in heraldry. The field, or background, has been painted white to represent the color silver. In this case, silver stands for the purity of the

paper before it has been drawn on. I used a lion because it is one of my favorite animals and because the lion is one of the earliest and most commonly used symbols in heraldry. It has been painted blue to denote sincerity. The lion is shown holding a quill, which represents the arts. The gold label in the upper right of the shield shows that I am a first-born son.

I decided to paint Merlin the way he is popularly portrayed—as an old man. However, some historians think that Merlin was no older than forty at the end of his recorded career. If you look closely at the painting of Merlin, you will see another parchment covered with wedge-shaped figures. These symbols are old English runes, part of an alphabet that was developed long before our own. If you are interested in deciphering Merlin's scroll, look at a hardcover edition of *The Hobbit* by J. R. R. Tolkien. Tolkien gives his readers hints on how to translate the runes. Good luck!

◇　◇　◇　◇　◇

SUGGESTED READING

I have made references to the legend of King Arthur—*Excalibur, Grail, Merlin, Round Table*—throughout this book. Did you know that there was a real King Arthur? Historians think that he lived in Britain in the fifth or sixth century. The vast body of Arthurian legend probably arose out of Celtic and Welsh tales from the sixth and seventh centuries. The legends were later expanded upon by Geoffrey of Monmouth, Layamon, Chrétien de Troyes, Sir Thomas Malory, and Tennyson, to name only a few! If you are interested in reading more about King Arthur and the knights of the Round Table, you might ask your librarian. My favorite books about King Arthur are:

The Arthurian Legends edited by Richard Barber
The Boy's King Arthur edited by Sidney Lanier
Stories of King Arthur and his Knights by Barbara Leonie Picard
The Story of King Arthur and his Knights by Howard Pyle
The Once and Future King and *The Book of Merlin* by T. H. White

—Jonathan Hunt

SELECTED BIBLIOGRAPHY

Cirker, Blanche, ed. *The Book of Kells: Selected Plates in Full Color.* New York: Dover Publications, 1982.

Cosman, Madeleine Pelner. *Medieval Holidays and Festivals.* New York: Charles Scribner's Sons, 1981.

Coulton, G. G. *The Medieval Scene: An Informal Introduction to the Middle Ages.* Cambridge: Cambridge University Press, 1959.

Day, David, and Alan Lee. *Castles.* New York: Bantam Books, 1984.

The Diagram Group. *Musical Instruments of the World.* New York: Paddington Press, 1976.

Gibson, Katherine. *The Goldsmith of Florence: A Book of Great Craftsmen.* New York: Macmillan, 1936.

Hogarth, Peter, and Val Cleary. *Dragons.* New York: Penguin Books, 1980.

Holmes, George, ed. *The Oxford Illustrated History of Medieval Europe.* Oxford and New York: Oxford University Press, 1988.

Levarie, Norma. *The Art and History of Books.* London: J. H. Heineman, 1968.

Macaulay, David. *Castle.* Boston: Houghton Mifflin, 1977.

Nordenfalk, Carl. *Early Medieval Book of Illumination.* New York: Rizzoli International Publications, 1988.

Onions, C. T., ed. *The Oxford Dictionary of English Etymology.* Oxford and New York: Oxford University Press, 1979.

Painter, Sidney. *French Chivalry: Chivalric Ideas and Practices in Medieval France.* Baltimore: The Johns Hopkins University Press, 1940.

—————. *A History of the Middle Ages.* New York: Alfred A. Knopf, 1953.

Reis, Reis, & Taylor. *Arthurian Legend and Literature.* Book I (The Middle Ages). New York: Garland Publishing, 1984.

Unterkircher, F., ed. *King René's Book of Love.* New York: George Braziller, 1980.

◇ ◇

I would like to thank Dr. Madeleine Pelner Cosman, Katherine Herzog, and, especially, Grace Chetwin for reading my original manuscript. Their knowledge, enthusiasm, and great love for all things medieval is appreciated.

First Aladdin Books edition 1993
Copyright © 1989 by Jonathan Hunt

Aladdin Books
Macmillan Publishing Company
866 Third Avenue
New York, NY 10022

Maxwell Macmillan Canada, Inc.
1200 Eglinton Avenue East, Suite 200
Don Mills, Ontario M3C 3N1

Macmillan Publishing Company is part of the Maxwell Communication Group of Companies.

Printed in the United States of America
10 9 8 7 6 5 4 3 2 1
The text of this book is set in Worcester Round. The initials are based on an alphabet from the twelfth century.

A hardcover edition of *Illuminations* is available from Bradbury Press, an affiliate of Macmillan, Inc.

Library of Congress Cataloging-in-Publication Data
Hunt, Jonathan. Illuminations / written and illustrated by Jonathan Hunt.—1st Aladdin Books ed. p. cm. Summary: A medieval alphabet book, illustrated in the style of illuminated manuscripts, presenting aspects of the Middle Ages from alchemist to zither.
ISBN 0-689-71700-8
1. Illumination of books and manuscripts, Medieval—Juvenile literature. 2. Middle Ages in art—Juvenile literature. [1. Civilization, Medieval. 2. Illumination of books and manuscripts, Medieval. 3. Alphabet.] I. Title.
ND2920.I44 1993 [E]—dc20 92-23542

◇ ◇

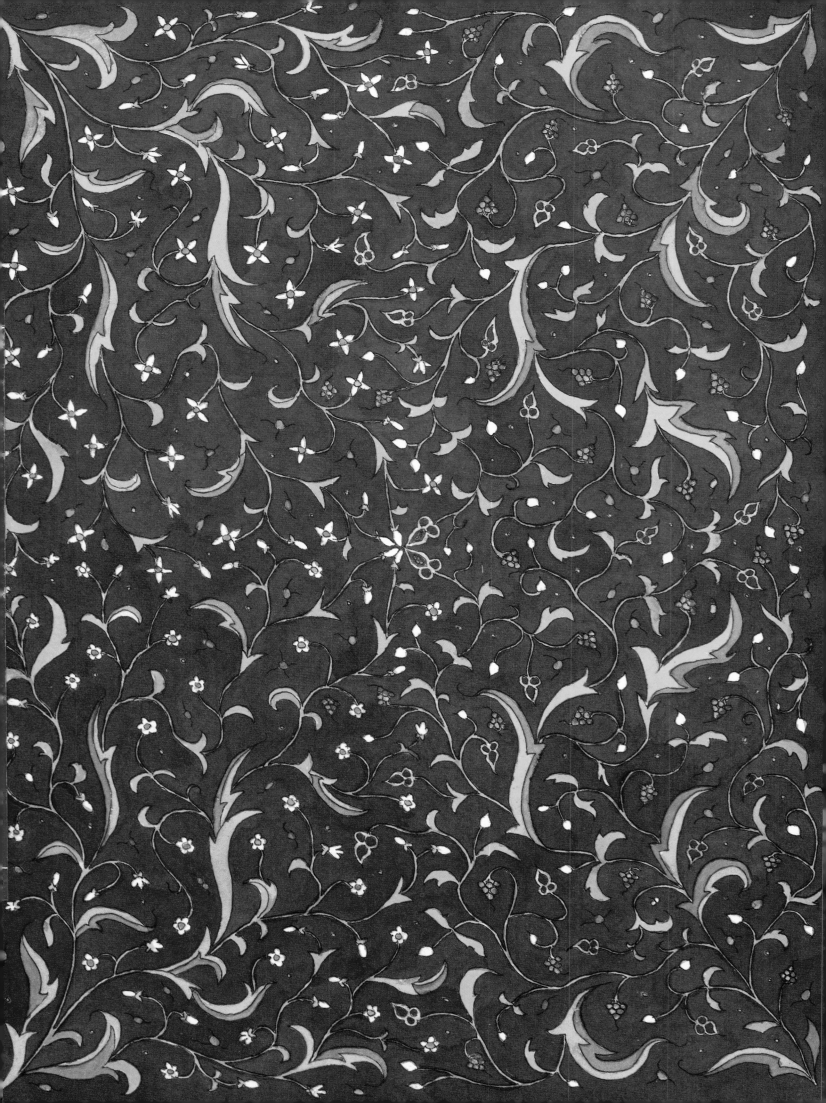

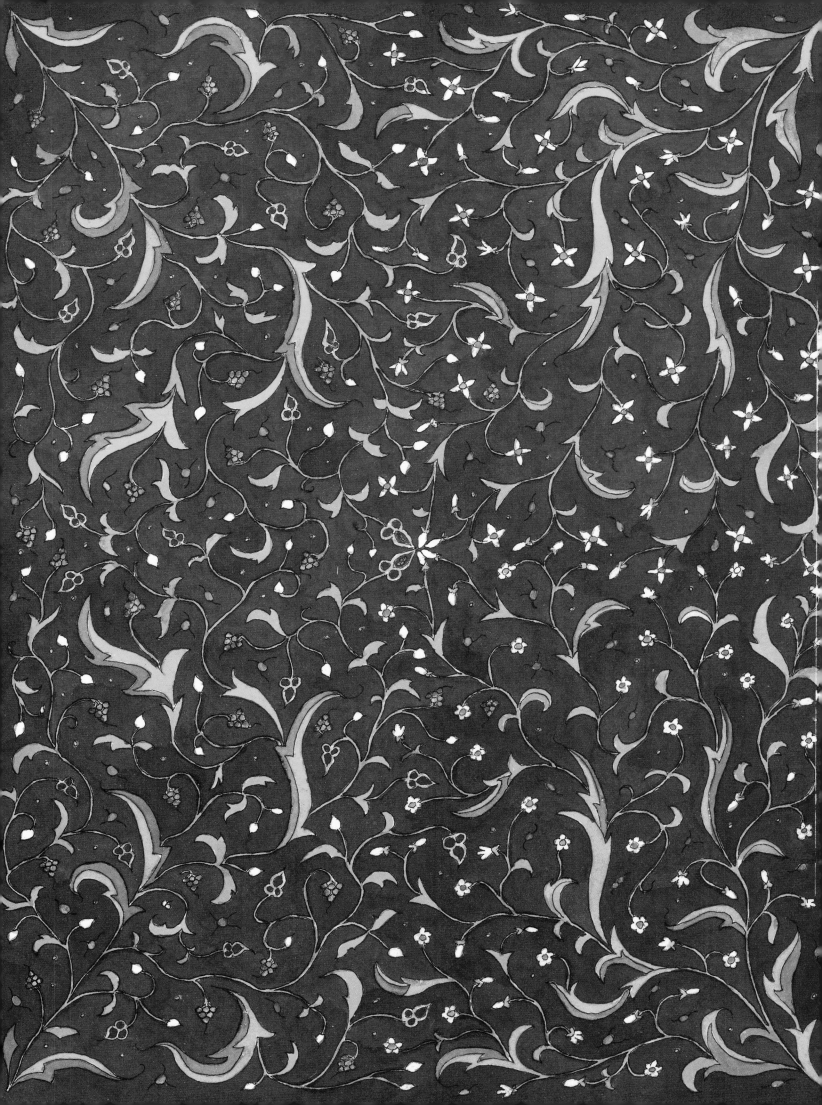

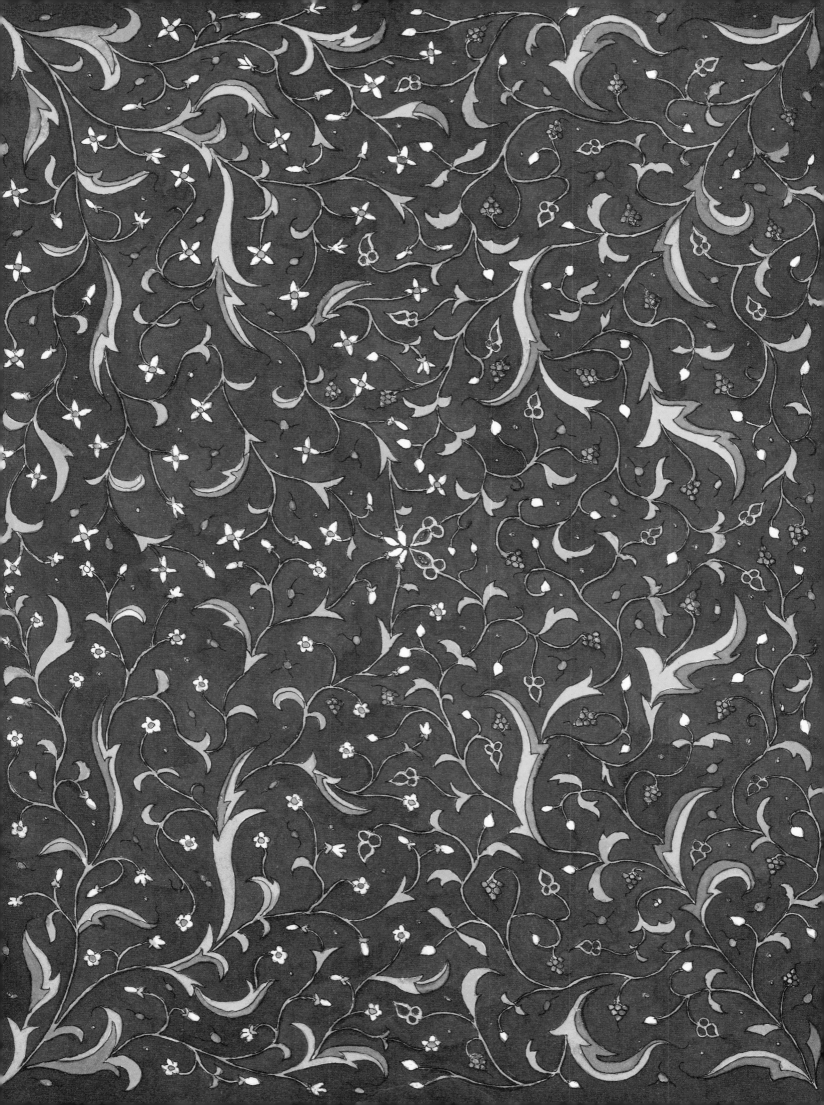